a
bear
and
his
boy

a bear and

by sean bryan

illustrations by tom murphy

his  boy

ARCADE PUBLISHING / NEW YORK

This is the story
of a bear named Mack,
who woke up one morning
with a boy on his back.

"Who are you?"

asked Mack,

to the kid on his back.

The boy
just shrugged
and replied,
"My name is Zach."

"Here's the deal," said the bear. "We've got no time to slack.

THINGS TO DO:
eat flapjacks
collect award
karate lesson
bird-watching
return books
work out
clean room
attend horse race
department store
finish jigsaw puzzle

do laundry
ballroom dancing
mow lawn
go kayaking
stop for ice cream
rent a movie
learn french
football game
try frozen yogurt
pierre's birthday
brush teeth

Just look at this schedule, it's totally packed.

First we're going to a diner to have some flapjacks.

Then it's off
to City Hall,
where I'm
accepting
a plaque.

Next we'll head to the gym to do ^{jumping} jacks,

and stop at the library
to browse
through
the
stacks.

We'll find an ice cream truck for an afternoon snack,

and then
watch the horses
race at the track!"

"**Whoa,**"
said the boy.
"You've got
a real knack
for running
around like
a maniac!"

"I know," said the bear, "I should be more laid-back, *but* . . .

the department store has a BIG SALE on slacks!

And
I've been
meaning
to try out
my new kayak.

Plus, it's Homecoming Weekend

and  we're quarterback!

"HOLD ON!"
yelled the boy.

The bear was taken aback.

"Let's stop
for a second and
smell the lilacs."

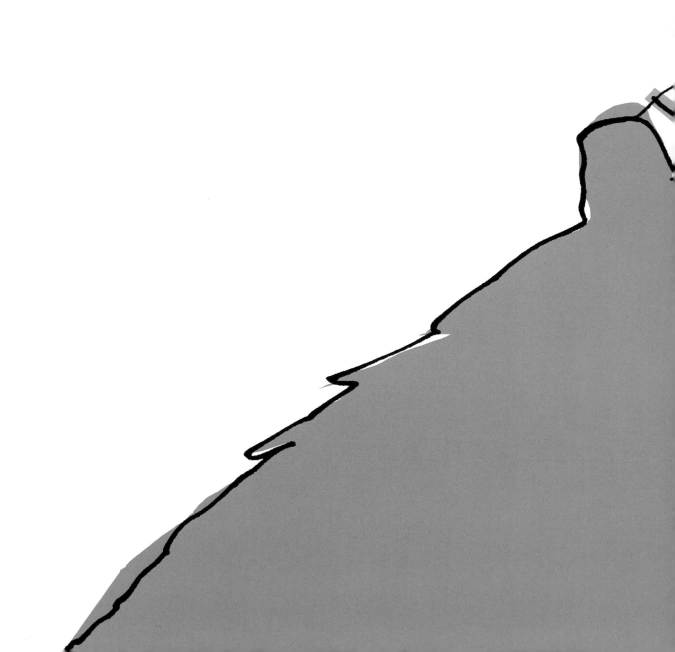

"How relaxing,"
said the bear.
"I should tell my friend Ned.

He's a stressed-out giraffe, with a girl on his head."

For my son, Ben, who has been on my head since 2004   — SB

For my nieces and nephews   — TM

FIRST EDITION

Library of Congress Cataloging-in-Publication Data
Bryan, Sean.
A bear and his boy / by Sean Bryan ; illustrated by Tom Murphy. —1st ed.
p. cm.
Summary: One morning, Mack the bear wakes up with Zach the boy on his back, but as Mack tries to complete a schedule that is "jam-packed," Zach suggests that he relax and take a second to smell the lilacs.
ISBN-13: 978-1-55970-838-8 (alk. paper)
ISBN-10: 1-55970-838-7 (alk. paper)
[1. Bears—Fiction. 2. Humorous stories. 3. Stories in rhyme.]
I. Murphy, Tom, 1972– ill. II. Title.

PZ8.3.B829Be 2007

[E]—dc22   2006037018

Published in the United States by Arcade Publishing, Inc., New York
Distributed by Hachette Book Group USA

Visit our Web site at www.arcadepub.com

10 9 8 7 6 5 4 3 2 1

Designed by Tom Murphy

IMAGO

Printed in Singapore

707
PS-G-2